Bungalo Books

Dedicated to the primary teachers who give children their first gentle push toward independent reading.

Written by Frank B. Edwards
Illustrated by John Bianchi
© 1998 by Bungalo Books

First printing 1998

Cataloguing in Publication Data

Edwards, Frank B., 1952-
   Is the spaghetti ready?

(Bungalo Books new reader series)
ISBN 0-921285-67-1 (bound)   ISBN 0-921285-66-3 (pbk.)

I. Bianchi, John   II. Title.   III. Title: Series

PS8559.D84I8 1998   jC813'.54   C97-901182-5
PZ7.E2535Is 1998

Published in Canada by: Trade Distribution:
Bungalo Books   Firefly Books Ltd.
Ste.100   3680 Victoria Park Ave.
17 Elk Court   Willowdale, Ontario
Kingston, Ontario   M2H 3K1
K7M 7A4

Co-published in U.S.A. by: Printed in Canada by:
Firefly Books (U.S.) Inc.   Friesen Printers
Ellicott Station   Altona, Manitoba
P.O. Box 1338   ROG OBO
Buffalo, New York
14205

Visit Bungalo Books on the Net at:
www.BungaloBooks.com

Send E-mail to Bungalo Books at:
Bungalo@cgocable.net

Is the Spaghetti Ready?

Written by Frank B. Edwards
Illustrated by John Bianchi

. . . french fries

. . . hot dog

. . . spaghetti

. . . pizza

I am hungry.
When can I eat?

Here is your food.
Now go to the table.

We are hungry.
When can we eat?

Here is your food.
Now go to the table.

We are hungry.
When can we eat?

Here is your food.
Now go to the table.

We are hungry.
When can we eat?

Here is your food.
Now go to the table.

Why are you not eating?

Now we can all eat together.

The End

The Author and Illustrator

Frank B. Edwards is a former writer and editor with Harrowsmith and Equinox magazines. John Bianchi is a cartoonist who works from his studio in Arizona's Sonoran Desert.

In 1986, they co-founded Bungalo Books and eventually gave up serious employment to create children's books on a full-time basis. They now have twenty-eight books to their credit.

John and Frank can be reached on the Internet at: bungalo@cgocable.net

Official Bungalo Reading Buddies

Kids who love to read books are eligible to become official, card-carrying Bungalo Reading Buddies. If you and your friends want to join an international club dedicated to having fun while reading, show this notice to your teacher or librarian. We'll send your class a great membership kit.

Teachers and Librarians

Bungalo Books would be pleased to send you a Reading Buddy membership kit that includes 30 full-colour, laminated membership cards. These pocket-sized, 2¼-by-4-inch membership cards can be incorporated into a wide variety of school and community reading programmes for primary, junior and intermediate elementary school students.

✳ **Each kit includes 30 membership cards, postcards, bookmarks, a current Bungalo Reading Buddy newsletter and a Bungalo storybook.**
✳ **Kits cost only $7.50 for postage and handling.**
✳ **No cash please. Make cheque or money order payable to Bungalo Books.**
✳ **Offer limited to libraries and schools.**
✳ **Please allow four weeks for delivery.**

Bungalo World Headquarters
17 Elk Court
Suite 100
Kingston, Ontario
K7M 7A4

Teachers and parents can visit Bunglo Books on the Net at: www.BungaloBooks.com